Dear Parents,

Welcome to the Scholastic Reader se
years of experience with teachers, pa   it
into a program that is designed to m
and skills.

> **Level 1**—Short sentences and stories made up of words kids
> can sound out using their phonics skills and words that are
> important to remember.

> **Level 2**—Longer sentences and stories with words kids need
> to know and new "big" words that they will want to know.

> **Level 3**—From sentences to paragraphs to longer stories, these
> books have large "chunks" of texts and are made up of a rich
> vocabulary.

> **Level 4**—First chapter books with more words and fewer
> pictures.

It is important that children learn to read well enough to succeed
in school and beyond. Here are ideas for reading this book with
your child:

- Look at the book together. Encourage your child to read the
  title and make a prediction about the story.
- Read the book together. Encourage your child to sound out
  words when appropriate. When your child struggles, you can
  help by providing the word.
- Encourage your child to retell the story. This is a great way
  to check for comprehension.
- Have your child take the fluency test on the last page to check
  progress.

Scholastic Readers are designed to support your child's efforts
to learn how to read at every age and every stage.
Enjoy helping your child learn to read and love to read.

> **—Francie Alexander**
> Chief Education Officer
> Scholastic Education

Library of Congress Cataloging-in-Publication Data

Augustyn, Brian.
  Batman : the Mad Hatter / by Brian Augustyn ; illustrated by Rick Burchett.
      p. cm. – (Scholastic reader. Level 3)
  "Batman created by Bob Kane."
  Summary: Batman meets and defeats the Mad Hatter.
  ISBN 0-439-47098-6 (pbk)
  [1. Heroes–Fiction. 2. Hats–Fiction. 3. Mystery and detective stories.]
  I. Burchett, Rick, ill. II. Title. III. Series.
PZ7.A9135 Bat 2004
[E]--dc22   2003021726
10 9 8 7 6 5 4 3 2 1   04 05 06 07 08

Printed in the U.S.A. 23 • First printing, March 2004

BATMAN™
THE MAD HATTER

Written by **Brian Augustyn**

Illustrated by **Rick Burchett**

Batman created by Bob Kane

Scholastic Reader — Level 3

Cartwheel
·B·O·O·K·S·®

SCHOLASTIC INC.

New York Toronto London Auckland Sydney
Mexico City New Delhi Hong Kong Buenos Aires

CHAPTER ONE

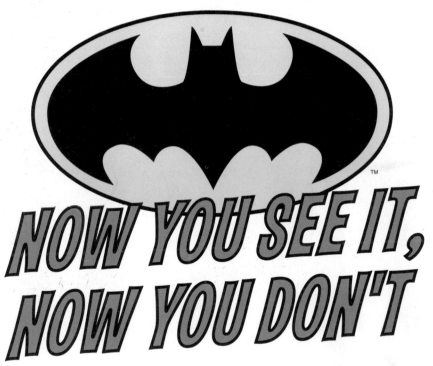

NOW YOU SEE IT, NOW YOU DON'T

Bruce Wayne was one of the richest men in Gotham City. He lived in Wayne Manor, above a secret cave — the Batcave!

That's because Bruce was also Batman!

Every evening, Batman carefully checked his crime-fighting tools and equipment. Then he would go out on patrol.

"Ice cream! Get your ice cream here!"

It was sunny in Gotham City today. And Benny Diaz was feeling happy.

Benny sold ice cream from a cart. He pushed the cart through the streets of downtown Gotham City.

Benny loved being outdoors.

He loved selling sweet treats to people.

Benny loved his clean white uniform.

Most of all, he loved his peaked cap. It was almost like an army officer's hat.

"I am a general in the Ice Cream Army," Benny thought, and he smiled.

Benny pushed his cart past Gotham Square Park. There he saw something tall. It was covered with a big cloth.

Under the cloth was the new Gotham Unity Monument. Benny had read about it in the newspaper. The monument had names on it of cities from all over the world.

On Friday, Gotham City was going to show off the monument. A special top piece would be added then. It would be made of glass. It would hold treasures from all those great cities. Benny liked this idea. He smiled wider.

Then a pretty blond young girl waved to

him. She wore a blue dress and a white apron. Benny thought she looked like Alice from *Alice in Wonderland*.

"I'd like a green ice pop, please," the girl said sweetly.

Not many people liked green ice pops. Benny bent over the cold box of his cart and felt his hat slip off his head.

He stood up with the green pop. But the pretty girl was gone. And so was Benny's beautiful white cap.

Benny was sad and puzzled. Why would anyone take his hat?

That evening, people all over Gotham City wondered the same thing.

A garbage man's cap disappeared while he emptied trash cans.

A bicycle messenger lost his helmet at a stop sign.

A policewoman's cap disappeared while she directed traffic.

A sewer worker, a tour guide, and a sign painter had all lost their hats that day, too.

Someone was stealing hats!

The people of Gotham City wondered why anyone would do that. They didn't know that one of the city's worst bad guys had returned.

The Mad Hatter!

CHAPTER TWO

ART HISTORY

A CROWD GATHERED BEHIND THE WATCHMAN...

STRANGE—BUT I *LIKE* IT!

It was now nighttime. In the Museum of Fine Art, a watchman was on duty. He stopped to look at his favorite painting. It was by an artist named René Magritte.

The painting showed a man wearing a black suit and a black hat. A large, green apple floated in front of the man's face.

"Strange—but I like it!" the watchman said to himself.

Behind him, four people gathered silently. The blond girl who had taken Benny Diaz's hat was there.

Two very large men stood beside her. They looked like twin giants in matching striped sweaters.

The fourth person was the Mad Hatter. He had a bushy mustache and a tall top hat. His smile beamed brightly.

The Mad Hatter tapped the watchman on the shoulder. As the watchman turned from the painting, he saw the Mad Hatter standing behind him.

Before the watchman could say a word, the Mad Hatter pressed a button on his hat. A bright yellow smoke squirted from inside. The watchman breathed it in and fell asleep.

Out on the street, a dark, powerful car

drove silently by the museum. A man with

a mask was inside the car. It was Batman!

He spoke into a two-way radio.

"This is Batman. There's a break-in at the

Museum of Fine Art. Send the police!"

Batman had heard about the hat thefts. He knew that the Mad Hatter was back to make trouble. And Batman was sure that he would find the villain inside the museum ... somewhere near the very famous and valuable painting with a hat!

Batman entered the museum with a key. The halls were dim. He moved quietly past statues and paintings. Soon Batman saw the Mad Hatter and his gang. They were stealing the painting of the man with the hat!

Batman pulled a small flashlight from his belt. He shone a bat-shaped light on the wall where the thieves worked. They jumped in surprise.

"It's Batman!" shouted the Mad Hatter. "Get him!"

BATMAN SHONE HIS BAT-LIGHT ON THE VILLAINS!

CHAPTER THREE

THE GREAT ESCAPE

The two big men moved to stop Batman.
Batman threw two capsules from his belt at
their feet. As the capsules broke, a shiny liquid
poured out.

It was oil, and the men slipped in it. They
fell down with a *BOOM!*

The Mad Hatter and the woman who
looked like Alice left the painting alone. They
ran to the center of the room. There they

stepped onto a large hat that lay on the floor.

Batman moved quickly. But the Mad Hatter's hat trick was even quicker. The hat lifted on large springs. The Mad Hatter and Alice bounced high into the air. They flew up and out a high window!

"Next time I won't be stopped!" the Mad Hatter shouted. "My next adventure will be my crowning glory!"

Batman watched them go. He knew he'd see them again.

The police took the two big men away. Outside the museum, Batman and Police Detective Renee Montoya spoke.

"These two are the Tweedle brothers, if you can believe it. Dee and Dominic," said Detective Montoya.

"Those names are perfect for the Mad

Hatter's Wonderland Gang," replied Batman. "He has an Alice, too."

Detective Montoya looked thoughtful. Something bothered her.

"Do you think the Mad Hatter stole all those different hats today just for practice?" she asked.

"Perhaps. The Mad Hatter likes stealing anything to do with hats," answered Batman. "Just like the painting tonight."

"Maybe it was his way of saying he was back," Montoya said with a smile.

"He's up to something. That's for sure. He said something about his 'crowning glory,'" said Batman.

He and the detective were silent. They were thinking.

"On Friday, the British Crown Jewels will

> BATMAN KNEW THE MAD HATTER WAS UP TO SOMETHING.

be at Gotham Center," said the detective. "And a crown is a kind of hat."

"That would attract the Mad Hatter all right," said Batman.

"The artist Magritte wanted people to see mysteries that are in plain sight. I think the Mad Hatter is telling us the same thing," he added. "We'll have to be ready for anything!"

CHAPTER FOUR

HAT TRICK

On Friday, Detective Montoya and many police officers were on guard at the Crown Jewels exhibit. Many people went to look at the fancy crowns. Gold and gems glittered in the bright lights.

There was no sign of the Mad Hatter and his gang. Still, the police waited. They were ready for anything.

At the same time, the Unity Monument was being unveiled across town.

Important people spoke. The crowd cheered. The large cloth was lifted off the monument.

"Gotham City dedicates this monument to world peace!" said Gotham's mayor. The crowd cheered louder.

A tall crane swung the top piece into place over the monument. Inside, the many treasures sparkled.

GOTHAM CITY'S *UNITY MONUMENT!*

MEANWHILE...

"This special capstone makes our wonderful monument even greater!" said the happy mayor.

Meanwhile, a man in an ice-cream vendor's uniform and cap pushed his cart through the crowd. He had a large and bushy mustache. He smiled as he looked up at the monument and its bright top.

Also in the crowd, a policewoman strolled by. She had long blond hair and looked a lot like Alice in Wonderland. She smiled, too.

A man in a sewer worker's hard hat climbed from a manhole. He moved toward the crane that held the capstone.

A bicycle messenger and a garbage man joined him. The three of them climbed into the crane's control cab.

"What the —" said the surprised crane

THE THREE MEN TIED UP THE CRANE OPERATOR.

operator. Before he could say more, the men tied him up.

Across the street, a sign painter in a beret looked up from his work and smiled. He had been sloppily painting a sign on a store door. Now he stopped.

The painter waved to a man driving a bus. The driver tipped his cap and drove forward. The big red bus bumped up onto the sidewalk and moved toward the monument.

The crowd cried out, "No! Watch out! Stop!" People began running when they saw the bus moving toward them. The ice-cream vendor hid his costume, tossed his white cap aside, and replaced it with a top hat. He was really the Mad Hatter! He chuckled nastily.

Then the Mad Hatter pulled a handful of hats from his cart. He tossed a flowered hat

toward the platform where the mayor stood with other important people. He tossed a baseball cap, too.

The hats squirted bright yellow smoke. The people close to the smoke fell asleep. Others ran away in fright.

"The treasure in the capstone is mine!" shouted the Mad Hatter. "No one can stop me!"

CHAPTER FIVE

HAT ENOUGH?

THE DARK KNIGHT TOWERED OVER THE MAD HATTER.

A deep voice called out from above, "Why do criminals always say that?"

The Mad Hatter looked around. Who had spoken?

It was Batman!

"Take the capstone, men!" the Mad Hatter

shouted angrily. "Leave this bothersome bat
to me!"

The Mad Hatter grabbed another of his
knockout hats and got ready to throw it. At
the same time, Batman swung down from a
nearby building on his Batrope. He grabbed the
large cloth that had covered the monument.

Batman tossed the cloth. It sailed down toward
the Mad Hatter. It covered him like a blanket.

"Let me out!" the Mad Hatter shouted. He
struggled, trapped underneath. But Batman
moved on.

BATMAN SWUNG TOWARD
THE MAD HATTER!

The Mad Hatter's men were lowering the monument's capstone onto the top of the bus. *THUMP!* Batman landed on the bus to stop them.

With a Batarang and his rope, Batman tied the men together. Then he left them dangling from the hook of the crane. "Help!" they shouted in fear. "Help!"

Back on the ground, the Mad Hatter finally came out from under the large cloth. His hat was crumpled. His hair and mustache were messy. And his suit was wrinkled and dirty.

The Mad Hatter knew his plan had failed! But he hoped he could still get away.

Suddenly, Batman was right next to him. Before the Mad Hatter could run, Batman grabbed the tall hat. He pulled down hard.

With the hat over his face, the Mad Hatter

BATMAN CAPTURED THE MAD HATTER WITH HIS OWN HAT!

couldn't see anything. There was no escape. Batman watched as the police arrested the villain.

"You were right, Batman," said Detective Montoya. "He was after the capstone."

"There had to be a reason to steal so many hats. If he was planning an indoor crime, why take so many outdoor hats?" Batman said. "And to the Mad Hatter, a capstone is a kind of hat."

"Well, you saved the monument! And we have the Mad Hatter and his gang," Detective Montoya said with a smile.

"Not quite the entire gang...." said Batman mysteriously.

CHAPTER SIX

PULLING THE WOOL OVER YOUR EYES

The girl who looked like Alice in Wonderland hurried away from Gotham Square.

Alice knew the Mad Hatter had been captured. She didn't want to be arrested, too! She was still dressed as a policewoman. So no one noticed her.

Suddenly, Alice's foot landed on something slippery. Her other foot skidded, too.

"Whoops!" Alice cried. She looked down as she fell. She had slipped on two green ice pops.

Nearby, Benny Diaz stood hatless and smiling. He was holding two ice-pop wrappers. Benny had recognized the girl who had stolen his hat. So he had come up with an idea. He had slid the pops under Alice's running feet so she would slip.

Seconds later, Batman arrived with the police. They thanked Benny for his help. And

WHOOPS!

BENNY'S PLAN HAD WORKED!

BATMAN GAVE BENNY HIS HAT BACK...

...AND THEN SWUNG OFF WITH A SMILE!

the police took Alice away.

Batman smiled and offered something to Benny. It was Benny's white cap. The Mad Hatter had tossed it into the crowd. And Batman had found it.

Benny smiled as he put the cap back on. He was in uniform again. And it felt great.

Then Batman swung off with a smile.

Benny Diaz loved his job. He was sure that Batman loved his job, too.

Fluency Fun

The words in each list below end in the same sounds.
Read the words in a list.
Read them again.
Read them faster.
Try to read all 15 words in one minute.

brightly	**brother**	**breathed**
carefully	**messenger**	**disappeared**
quickly	**officer**	**poured**
silently	**painter**	**returned**
sweetly	**wrapper**	**wrinkled**

Look for these words in the story.

museum	**liquid**	**monument**
beautiful	**uniform**	

Note to Parents:

According to *A Dictionary of Reading and Related Terms*, fluency is "the ability to read smoothly, easily, and readily with freedom from word-recognition problems." Fluency is necessary for good comprehension and enjoyable reading. The activities on this page include a speed drill and a sight-recognition drill. Speed drills build fluency because they help students rapidly recognize common syllables and spelling patterns in words, and they're fun! Sight-recognition drills help students smoothly and accurately recognize words. Practice these activities with your child to help him or her become a fluent reader.

—**Wiley Blevins,**
Reading Specialist